Rhymes About Us

Rhymes About Us

Marchette Chute

illustrations by the author

E. P. DUTTON & CO., INC.   NEW YORK

Library of Congress Cataloging in Publication Data

Chute, Marchette Gaylord   Rhymes about us

SUMMARY: A collection of poems about familiar experiences,
emotions, and events of childhood, such as getting a new
pair of shoes or having a bad day.

[1. American poetry]   I. Title.

PZ8.3.C477RM   811'.5'2   74-4272   ISBN 0-525-38220-8

Published simultaneously in Canada by Clarke,
Irwin & Company Limited, Toronto and Vancouver

Designed by Riki Levinson
Printed in the U.S.A.   First Edition
10 9 8 7 6 5 4 3 2 1

For Joy

Contents

Morning

How pleasant it is
  To see the light
Come in the window
  And push out the night.

How splendid it is
  To hear someone say
There will be pancakes
  For breakfast today.

1

Words

I like to listen to the sound
Of bells and tunes and birds.
I also like the special sound
You sometimes get in words
Like "crash" and "slithery" and "pop"
And "murmuring" and "clang"
And "tinkle" and that lovely word
That simply goes off "bang!"

An Event

Something's happened very fine.
   New shoes.
   Guess whose?
Mine!

My Little Dog

My little dog is dear to me.
He has no faults that I can see.

He is the finest dog I know
And I quite often tell him so.

Dinnertime

I am told
   To sit up nicely.
I am told
   I should not stuff
All my dinner
   In a minute
And three helpings
   Are enough.

No one says,
   "Do have another.
You can hardly
   Stop at three."
No one wants
   Me to be happy
In the way
   I want to be.

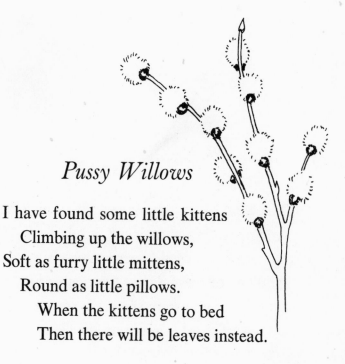

Pussy Willows

I have found some little kittens
  Climbing up the willows,
Soft as furry little mittens,
  Round as little pillows.
    When the kittens go to bed
    Then there will be leaves instead.

The Swing

The wind blows strong and the swing rides free,
And up in the swing is me, is me,
  And the world goes rushing by,
And one of these days I'll swing so far
I'll go way up where the sea birds are
  And plant my feet on the sky.

My Teddy Bear

A teddy bear is a faithful friend.
You can pick him up at either end.
His fur is the color of breakfast toast,
And he's always there when you need him most.

Valentine

I'll make a card for my Valentine,
Lacy center and golden twine,
Cut red paper for a heart
(This is quite the hardest part).
Then I'll have to think of who
I would like to give it to.

Planning

I plan to go a walk today
   And so I think I'd better
Make up a pile of things I need.
   I'll take along a sweater
In case it's cold. I'll take a cap
   In case it should be sunny.
I'll take along a dime or two
   In case I need some money.
I'll need to take a lot of lunch
   Because there is no knowing
If there will be some things to eat
   At where I may be going.
I'll take some sandwiches with me,
   Some candy bars for chewing,
Some apples and a piece of cake.
   It takes a lot of doing
To gather up the many things
   I have to find or borrow.
Perhaps I'll make my plans today
   And take my walk tomorrow.

Learning to Swim

Swimming is an easy thing
   If you know how to do it.
You push the water wide apart
   And then you just go through it.

Refuge

I sit here so still in my secret place,
   So still and so quiet I be,
That even the quietest sort of a leaf
   Could not be more silent than me.

Crayons

I've colored a picture with crayons.
　　I'm not very pleased with the sun.
I'd like it much stronger and brighter
　　And more like the actual one.
I've tried with the crayon that's yellow,
　　I've tried with the crayon that's red.
But none of it looks like the sunlight
　　I carry around in my head.

Contentment

I would like to be wise,
    I would like to be strong,
I would like to be right
    And never be wrong.
But since none of this
    Is likely to be,
I'm really quite happy
    To be only me.

Neighbors

If I lie down flat where the tall grass grows
    I can watch all the passersby—
The ants, the spiders, and other small things
    That creep and that run and that fly.

As long as I stay very quiet and still
    They do not mind if I stare.
They like to have me down in the grass
    Watching their travels there.

The Wrong Start

I got up this morning and meant to be good,
But things didn't happen the way that they should.

    I lost my toothbrush,
        I slammed the door,
    I dropped an egg
        On the kitchen floor,
    I spilled some sugar
        And after that
    I tried to hurry
        And tripped on the cat.

Things may get better. I don't know when.
I think I'll go back and start over again.

The Beginning of Spring

The buds on the trees at this time of the year
   Are so tightly and carefully curled,
It's hard to believe an astonishing thing—
   The greenness they'll bring to the world.

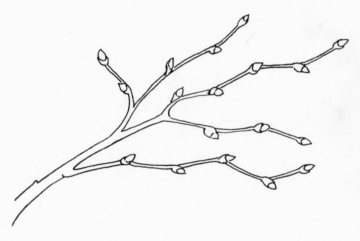

Showers

   Squelch and squirt and squiggle,
   Drizzle and drip and drain—
   Such a lot of water
   Comes down with the rain!

A Problem

My zipper is stuck
  And what shall I do?
Give it a jerk
  And break it in two,
Give it a tug
  And then it will jam—
I think I'll just sit here
  The way that I am.

The Visitor

Everyone had a chance to see
The baby owl in the apple tree.
When it was dark he flew away,
But he was here all yesterday.

Wanting

What I want right now is a watch of my own.
I don't want to wait until I'm grown.
I don't want to wait another day.
I want it now in the strongest way.

If people knew how I felt about it,
They wouldn't let me be without it.
They'd say, "Well, well," and "Yes, we see,"
And hurry to bring my watch to me.

The Surprise

I had a pollywog with a tail.
It lived alone in its little pail
Until one day it suddenly grew,
And I have the frog it turned into.

Reasons

The reason for a lawn
    Is to sit down upon it.
The reason for a cake
    Is to pile frosting on it.
The reason for the sun
    Is to shine down on me,
But spelling has no reason
    As far as I can see.

(Afterthought)

I wasn't fair to spelling.
    It has its reasons too.
It is the way you recognize
The words you read if you are wise,
For each word has its shape and size
    Just like your neighbors do.

My Little Brother

He does not always do or think
  Or say just what he should.
He is as good as he can be,
  But that's not very good.

Winter Night

As I lie in bed I hear
The east wind crying in my ear,
And soon will follow, soft and low,
The sifting whisper of the snow.

Journey

The snow is deep
   And the sun has set,
My nose is cold
   And my feet are wet,

But I'll soon be home
   And there will be
A cup of cocoa
   Waiting for me,

A place to sit
   And warm my feet,
And bread and butter
   For me to eat.

My Fishes

My goldfish swim like bits of light,
Silver and red and gold and white.
They flick their tails for joy, and then
They swim around the bowl again.

Reading

A story is a special thing.
    The ones that I have read,
They do not stay inside the books.
    They stay inside my head.

In the Night

When I wake up and it is dark
    And very far from day
I sing a humming sort of tune
    To pass the time away.

I hum it loud, I hum it soft,
    I hum it low and deep,
And by the time I'm out of breath
    I've hummed myself to sleep.

My Kitten

Kitten, my kitten,
  Soft and dear,
I am so glad
  That we are here
Sitting together
  Just us two
You loving me
  And me loving you.

Boating

Anything does for a ship if it floats,
But a milkweed pod is the best of boats.

A toothpick mast and a paper sail
Help it to weather the strongest gale,

And if it tangles with water weeds
A bit of pushing is all it needs.

Night Travel

Two things fly in the dark of the night
And carry with them a lovely light.
>One is the firefly,
>>Low in the grasses,
>The other the aeroplane
>>Up where it passes.

Bats fly, too, and owls can roam,
But they have no light to light them home.

My Family

Part of my family is grown-up and tall.
Part of my family is little and small.
I'm in the middle and pleased with them all.

The New Muffler

Muffled in my muffler,
   Striding through the snow,
I am much admired
   Everywhere I go.

Eating Out in Autumn

Deep in the woods is a blackberry bush
    And the berries are waiting there,
Juicy and round and shining black
    For me and the birds to share.

Deep in the woods is a wild grape vine
    And the grapes so secret grow
That only the mice and a squirrel or two
    (And me, of course) can know.

Oh, spring is good and summer is fine,
    But the very best time is fall.
I could live all day in the wild, wild woods
    And never come out at all.

Advice

"Come along, come along,
   Don't take all day.
Hurry up, hurry up,"
   That's what they say.

"What are you doing
   With everyone gone,
Sitting and thinking,
   Your stocking half on?"

"Come along, come along,
   Don't be so slow."
That's what they tell me
   Wherever I go.

Rabbits

I went very quietly
   Over the ground
And three baby rabbits
   Is what I found,
Safe in a meadow
   Where no one could see,
No one could find them
   Except only me,
Tucked in the grasses
   So careful and neat.
Oh, their dear little ears
   And their sweet little feet!

The Hot Day

If I were butter I would melt,
    It is so hot today.
In fact, most people seem to think
    It's just too hot to play.

Since I have nothing else to do
    I think that I will break
An egg upon the pavement here
    To see if it will bake.

No one has ever thought of this.
    It might, as like as not,
Be just the way to cook an egg
    When it's so very hot.

School Concert

My family was the very proudest.
They said my singing was the loudest.

One Day Only

I answered back today in school.
I put a frog in the swimming pool.
I stole a cake that was left to cool.
No, I didn't.
    April Fool!

At the Library

This is a lovely place to be.
  The books are everywhere,
And I can read them here, or take
  Them home and read them there.

It is a kind of secret place
  Where I can enter in
And no one tells me where to stop
  Or where I should begin.

The books sit waiting on their shelves,
  As friendly as can be,
And since I am a borrower
  They all belong to me.

Cookies

If I had a kitchen
    And knew how to bake,
These are the cookies
    I would make:
Chocolate, peanut,
    Lemon and spice—
All the ones
    That are extra nice.
And to everyone on the block I'd say,
"Here are the cookies I made today.
Come and eat them right away."

Opportunity

Somewhere I have lost my shoe.
Don't know what I ought to do.
I could go and tell my mother,
Or, better yet, I could lose the other.

Politeness

I met a squirrel the other day
And spoke to him in a friendly way.
I couldn't pat him on the head
But I gave him several nuts instead.
He took them from me one by one
And waved his tail when he was done,
And he was happy, I could tell.

We both behaved extremely well.

The Muddle

In the middle of the muddle is me.
It's a place where I am very apt to be.
I get myself all straightened out
    And then
I'm right back in the muddle
    Again.

Bedtime

I like the things that come at night—
Being tickled; a pillow fight;
Hearing stories told in bed,
Or perhaps a chapter read;

Drinks of water, two or three,
And my puppy close to me.

Getting About

Walking is slower and not so much fun.
Sensible children usually run.

On the Sidewalk

I may decide to leave this street
And climb up on a steeple.
I think I've seen about enough
Of just the legs of people.

Spring Saturday

It shouldn't start to rain today.
I want to go outdoors and play.
The proper time to rain is when
It's Monday morning back again.

Losing Mittens

I'm always losing mittens.
　I had them on a string.
I even tried a pair of clips.
　I can't do anything
　　To keep them where they ought to be.
　　They really are a trial to me.

A Dream of Wildflower Names

In the place where I have gone
There's lady's bedstraw to sleep upon,
Moccasin flowers for my feet,
Shepherd's purse to keep things neat,
Queen Anne's lace and thimble weed
For the sewing that I need,
And if there should be a storm
Fireweed to keep me warm.

Making a Home

I don't happen
 To be a mouse,
But if I were
 I would build my house
Where the rushes grow
 By the waterside
And baby things
 Can safely hide,
And all my mouselings,
 Warm and dry,
Could watch the river
 As it goes by.

A Growl

If I were full of cheerfulness
    I would go out and play,
But I am feeling rather cross
    So I'll stay home today.
Tomorrow I will like my friends.
    Today I really don't.
So I'll stay home and please myself
    Since other people won't.

Seasons

Cherries and roses,
　Swimming and bees,
Summer's the season
　For things like these.

Skating and snowballs,
　Too many clothes,
Winter's the season
　For things like those.

The Outdoor Christmas Tree

Suet chunks and popcorn strings,
Cranberry chains and apple rings,
Bits of corn and sunflower seeds,
Everything a bluejay needs
Or an anxious chickadee—
Come and see it. Come and see!

Sleeping Outdoors

Under the dark is a star,
Under the star is a tree,
Under the tree is a blanket,
And under the blanket is me.

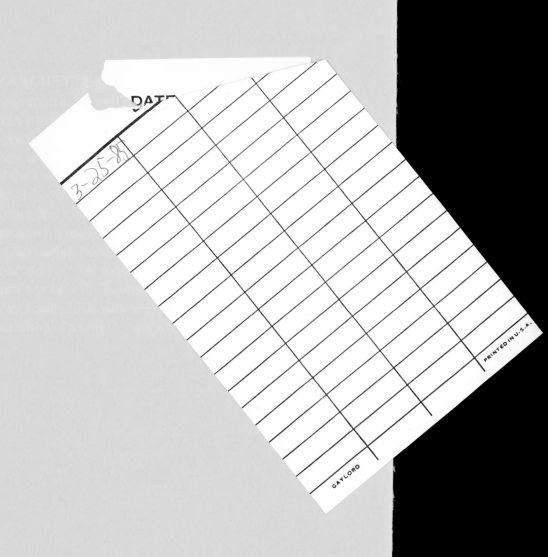

DATE

3-25-85

GAYLORD

PRINTED IN U.S.A.